Her Unbroken Soul

PUBLISHED BY

Her Unbroken Soul

Compiler

Falha Khan

Falha Khan is in 8th standard studying in St. Paul's Senior Secondary School. She is from Rampur, Uttar Pradesh. She is of 13 years old. Since from her childhood she loves to read and write. For her "Words have more power than the poem ever has". She is a Published co-author in more than 15 books. She wants to be a Published author and now for this, she is writing her solo book.

Say bye

Above the land

Below the sky

Counting the stars,

And you are mine.

Hold my hand,

And never leave it until I die.

What if I mix with sand?

And say bye.

Falha Khan

Index

PROBLEMS ARE THE SOLUTIONS

Problems are the solutions

to freshen your mind.

Get problems and get solutions,

are the answers to find.

Having trouble in your path to success

doesn't mean you lose,

Just go up and up,

And try the road to cross.

Problems are the solutions

to freshen your mind.

Get problems and get solutions

are the answers to find.

Falha Khan

INHALE POSITIVITY AND EXHALE_NEGATIVITY

All you require is

Positive mind and

Positive people

to explain

Negative mind and

Negative people

We can overcome from you.

Just wait and watch.

Abha Bindal

फूल और खुशबू के स्वप्न।

खुशबू ने एक दिन फूल से ये कहा,

मैं एक धुन बनू तुम बंसी बनो,

मैं घनश्याम बनू तुम राधिका बनो,

मैं तो प्रेमी बनू तुम प्रेमिका बनो। (१)

फूल ने खुशबू से ये उत्तर दिया,

मैं हकीक़त बनू तुम सपना बनो,

मैं चाहत बनू तुम ईप्शा बनो,

मैं रती बनू तुम कामदेव बनो। (२)

खुशबू ने फूल से मुस्कुराके कहा,

मैं प्राण बनू तुम शरीर बनो,

मैं दीपक बनू तुम दीवाली बनो,

मैं तो रंग बनू तुम होली बनो। (३)

फूल ने खुशबू से मुस्कुराके कहा,

मैं जुगनू बनू तुम अंधेरा बनो,

मैं सूरज बनू तुम किरण बनो,

मैं कवि बनू तुम भावना बनो। (४)

Akash Barik

FATE

Meeting you in solace was fate,

My soul wished to enter your heart's gate,

Loving you is my choice till date,

But I guess I had been just playing date.

Ankit Singh

ENGRAVED

I sat there at a coffee shop sipping on a warm mug of hot chocolate. The light pattering of raindrops on the pavement and "Us" by James Bay playing in the shop. I was completely immersed in my book, unaware of my surroundings. Suddenly, I felt a presence sit in front of me. I looked up from my book and was met with a lad of beautiful green eyes looking straight at me. His dark brown locks almost covering his eyes.

"You're beautiful" he said under his breath. I was surprised at his statement and thought I heard him wrong.

"Pardon", I said, "Were you saying something?"

"I said you're beautiful", he said, looking deep into my eyes while smiling. And my heart skipped a beat. That usually happens when someone you have a major crush on says something so sweet or when a handsome man compliments you.

I looked at him with my face a little pink dusted on my cheeks. "Thank you", I said after a few seconds.

It was a little weird because we had just met and we both were looking into each other's souls.

"Can I take you out on a date tomorrow?", he asked. For a moment I got lost in his deep and husky voice. "We just met, sir. I don't even know your name", I replied, chuckling. "Then say yes. We'll get a chance to know each other. And my name is Jeremy." He came a little closer to me and again looked deep in my eyes as if he'd find his answer there. "okay" I said, laughing.

At that time, I didn't know what I was signing up for but I'm glad that I did. Because from that day on he gave me a dream of a forever.

< 3years later >

Even though 3 years have passed it still seems like yesterday when I met him in this very coffee shop. I was sitting in the exact spot all those years ago. But this time when I looked out the window, I could see the golden sun rays of the summer sun and him walking towards me with his beautiful brown locks shining in the sunlight. He entered the coffee shop, looked at me and gave me his beautiful bright smile and handed me a small bouquet of sunflowers and held my hands. He again looked at me with his gorgeous green eyes, and as always, I found myself getting lost in them.

He softly started, "the day we first met, I saw you from a distance immersed in your book. Something about you attracted me and it still does. And when my eyes first met yours, I couldn't help but lose myself in those hazel eyes. Now I can't find an escape from their depths. So, will you do the honour of keeping my heart locked in your tender hands, safe and sound for the rest of our lives?"

Tears pricked my eyes, "yes, I will." He took me in his arms and held me tight and at that moment I was happy that I agreed to go on a date with this stranger who eventually became my forever.

Ankita Suman Barla

GRAVELLED TRUST

All the eye bags

All the lies,

All the innocence & the Petechiae

Hidden behind the makeup folds,

Thinning scars on her cranium,

Emotions in her eye's fathoms deep,

Lips covered with flashing gloss,

Seeking admiration,

For signs of mutilation,

Such brokenness on resting scars,

Impressions of a few dirty hands,

Painted along her leased body

Collapsing soul, hideous sobs,

A tease to be called, burning in hell fire,

Streams of blood stroking down,

Tired of his sadistic games,

Finding herself stretching into the direction of
sunny rays

Just a missed step leading downstairs,

Liqueur infused air and a broken neck,

A scag in one, booze in the other

Her hands home to lazing scars

"Mirror, Mirror, on the wall,

Am I the fairest of them all?",

Lying dead on the floor,

Seeking validation

With all the mutilation,

Picturing a perfect, porcelain doll,

''Mirror, Mirror, on the wall,

Tell me who is the fairest of them all.''

Areeba Asif

LOVE

I love you because you actually put effort into me.

I love you because nobody has ever given me the
love that you have given me and you are the only
one that could ever love me this way.

I love you because you always make me feel that I
am worth something.

I love you because you have a nurturing nature and
you take care of me.

I love you because you made me smile when I
almost forgotten how to.

I love because you have a huge and honest heart.

I love you and everything like detail about you.

I love you because you are simply you.

Ashima Jain

DILEMMA OF LOVE

I was searching for you, I wanted to see you.

I was thinking of you, I wanted to be with you.

I was trying to get you, I wanted us for forever.

But there were Consequences as

I was loving you from my heart, and you wanted the lust.

I wanted us for eternity and you wanted us for option.

There's a dilemma between love and happiness, and I chose happiness for eternity.

Asmita Ahuja

LOVE AND DREAMS

Love and Dreams

I have first-hand belief that someday

you will get off

from a new chocolate bar

to touch my soul

with your dewy delicate hands

of motherly love...

You may stay in the cozy

ambience of the hut I made

with the reeds of my blood,

My love is a paradox

with shiny snows...

How can you survey the deeper warmth

of my love and dreams

that eat up the pains of the wounded world?

Ayushi Tiwari

LOVE

Deserted are those nights I lay awake in a bed alone
whisked away from the love I was suckling from
your lips only hours ago.

Whisked so fast from your warm embrace,

Enveloping my entirety in a same way your hot
mouth wraps around my tongue.

What I'd give

To have you leaning above me,

Propped up on your hands

With your body stretched across the mattress like a
highway overpass.

With your dark eyes glimmering like street lights on
wet asphalt, and your hair swinging in your face.

Like telephone wires

You are an entire city

The hum of your breath in your chest

Like subway trains ripping through the underground

The rumble of your groan echoing from behind your
ribs, shaking the grated sidewalks beneath my feet.

Your laughter,

Electrifying

Like digital billboards and neon lights

Flashing back and forth across the skyline

Your cry like emergency sirens fleeing through the
streets

And your beautiful mouth hanging open softly,

The Stark contrast to the sandpaper grin rising from
your stubbly chin.

Like a flower growing through the cracks in the
concrete, with your pink mouth and chipped teeth.

I want to crawl inside your body and make a home
there

Leave my things strew across the floor

Open the windows to let in the breeze

And throw myself down onto the soft with a content
sigh.

I LOVE YOU TIRELESSLY

Baisakhi Das

MERE KHWAABO KI BAARAT

Mujhe pyaar me ishq chahiye ,

Mujhe ruh me ruaab chahiye,

Mujhe dushman me dosti chahiye,

Mujhe insaan me insaaniyat chahiye,

Mujhe dil me padi ek diwaar chahiye,

Mujhe vo ladkiyan chahiyen jo samaj ko piche rakh
aage badti ho.

Mujhe pyaar me ishq chahiye,

Mujhe vo ladke chahiye jo ladki ko dekh use apni
behen ka aadar de.

Mujhe is jahan me insaaniyat chahiye,

Vo dil lagi chahiye jispe kisika hak na ho,

Muje pyaar me ishq chahiye.

Bhavini Ramesh Dhuva

WISH IF HE IS MINE

He is marvel beyond words and time,

From his breath to beats he is only mine.

He smells like goodness and glee,

Of my morning coffee and evening tea.

His eyes are deep and brown as calm as the sea,

For me he is my honey and I am her bee.

He feels like laughter like sadness and pain,

But he keeps me alive and sane.

He is so perfect unlike me unlike you,

Sometimes it makes me wonder if he is true.

We always love at night,

Sometimes we do fun, sometimes we fight.

I always miss his memories at nine.

I wish if he could be mine.

He loves like romeo , ranjha and majnu,

But not me he loves another like u.

Chavi Mehra

टूटने के बाद भी जिंदा रहकर

मंज़िल पाने की चाहत

रातों के अंधेरों से अब वो डरा नहीं करती

बंदिश की बेड़ियों से खुद को जकड़ा नहीं करती ,

बनना चाहतीं हैं वो टूटने के बाद भी चमकता हुआ तारा ,

ए ! खुदार जमाने ,वो स्त्री बार- बार जन्मा नहीं करती।

कहते हैं बुरा भला तो कहने दो उन्हें

बोलना उनकी आदत,

उनको क्षमा करना मेरी जरूरत हैं फिलहाल

हकीक़त बदलने की कामना करने वाली

अपनी हिम्मत और हौसले पर विश्वास रखने वाली,

कठिन कसौटियों को पार कर जाने वाली,

अपनी मंज़िल से जुदा हुआ नहीं करती।

मुंह फेर लेते हैं वो, जो मुझे कभी अपना सगा कहा करते थे,

पैगाम तो टूटने पर अपने भी भेजा नहीं करते।

हँसते - हँसते उस दर्द के विष को पी जाने वाली

ज़िंदा रहने की चाहत रखने वाली,

इतिहास के पन्नों की मशहूर रचना बना करती हैं

लेकिन कभी आम मौत मरा नहीं करती।

Chinsha Bhatia

LET'S DROP

Love of droplets with Plants.

Let's Drop

Why these delicate strings still hold me?

Even if they can tear apart by my single extra drop.

Feels so delighted, I am weaved along their web,
having such a greenery lap.

Sometimes I wonder people won't value me if I am
in abundance.

But this small web holds me like every drop values.

I wish I could be with them feeling my every drop
owns a green and comfy lap.

Sometimes you need to risk yourself at your
weakest section.

Trust me you will feel the strongest.

Alike this web, one string in your life will hold you
and will never let you fall.

That's your inner conscience and inner will.

This is my story as my title says Let's drop and dance.

Yours Droplet

Devyani Neral

DURR HOKAR BHI HAMESHA PAAS

Sabhi ne babu, shona, cutie kiya hoga apni zindagi mein ek na ek baar. Mera matlab ye hai ki aap ek baar toh relation mein rahe honge. Sabhi ne kia hoga pyar! Karna toh aasan hai par nibhana bhut mushkil. Ek dusre ka khayal rakhna, khudse jyaada apne pyar ka khayal rakhna, uski baahon mein sara jahan paana, usse durr jaane se gabrana, uske galat hone pr bhi uska saath na chorna, shayad yahi hai sacha pyar. Par achanak ye sab khatam ho jaye toh. Ji main breakup ki baat nahi kar rahi, main long distance relationship ki baat kar rhi hoon. Jisse hum milla karte the ,roz baat kia karte the, usse ek din bhi durr jaane par gabraya karte the, toh socho aaj hum mein kitni himmat hai jo hum unse itne durr hai, na kuch baat hoti hai, na phones , kuch nai par beintehaan pyar,

Kya kar sakts hai hame apne sapnebhi toh purre karne hai, agar woh sache honge, saath aage bhi nibhana chahenge , toh jaroor laut jayenge. Aur kisne keh diya ki pyar purra nai hota, agar kismat mein hoga aur pyar beshumaar hoga toh zaroor purra hoga. Toh kya hua aaj nahi huyi hamari baat, toh kya hua aaj nahi huyi hamari mulaakat, par aap hi rahenge hamare liye khaaz, aap ke hi liye honge hamesha hamare jazbaat.

Diksha Motwani

THE PORTRAIT OF LOVE

Love is the final mourn of every heart,

Every heart pulsates at being typically insomniac.

It nests and frees; gives and receives,

Entirety to the universe.

Love is the greenery on the face of the earth,

Pregnant clouds in the turf,

Those conceive the visions of hopeful likelihood,

And a reason to believe, that

The earth is a bower of abundant godliness.

Love is the beauty that dazzles the stars,

Restful illumination of the heaven afar,

That perceives the acts of sins and saints alike,

And designs a treason to weave, that

The earth is a refugee plenty of humanness.

Love is the music that reverberates the galaxies,

Diversified orbits where harmoniously exist,

That deceive the endeavour of million meteors,

And form a liaison to cleave, that

The earth is an abode of beautiful togetherness.

Love is the sacrifice that the earth does,

Torn and ploughed but never departs,

That receives and imbibes the infinite wounds,

And masons to heave endless ground, that

The earth is a seed of ardent amiableness.

Oh! my love,

Love is the depth of oceanic amount,

Fathomless and countless account;

Of care, of need

Of respect indeed.

That I realise in your pulse,

And I go vagrant universal.

Dipu Sharma

THE DARK'S LOVE

In the darkling night,

When people are dreaming around,

I look up at the sky,

To see those stars,

Which speaks stories to me.

With that shining moon,

I try to sing lullaby,

Stars giving me the chorus,

Under those dark spread sheets,

Every night on my terrace.

Living amidst of the chaos,

And phantom spread emotions,

Running away from all those things,

She seeks solace in those stars,

With peace in that silent winds.

Breaking down the hurdles,

Diving deep from the grudges,

Standing strong to the stormy nights,

She is trying to love herself deeper,

Everyday better than yesterday's chapter.

G. Nagavaishnavi

SORRY, I CAN'T BEAR THIS ANYMORE

You broke me,

I suffered from depression for 2 years or more,

Now, I couldn't bear the pain anymore.

One more chance,

You do not deserve.

But I will give it to you anyway,

Because what's the effect of one more crack in the
glass.

What's the effect of one more scar on my soul?

I want to say you that,

"Your voice was like a sweet song,

Your hug was a sigh of relief to me,

Your slow kisses were the most beautiful gestures
for me.

Stay with me, I'm still in love with you.

Don't leave my heart lying here with nobody left to
lose.

You know those things we never had the chance to
do.

Be with me now and forever my love."

But sorry I can't bear this anymore,

I told you I didn't do anything wrong,

Yet you believed their lies all along

I was the love of your life remember?

You promised to cherish me forever.

One mistake - and not even on my part,

Tales told viciously just to break my heart

I was on my knees,

I begged you to listen to my soulful cries.

Tell me frankly, what did I ever do to you?

You don't have any reason right...?

And now you are asking for a second chance?

Garima Jain

THE NEW COSMOS 2020

This is the 21st century: a century which is still manufacturing a world of difference via the New, Innovative and Modern generation.

An era, which is developing in almost all aspects of fields, then be that from Science and technology, nuclear missiles, economic growth, trade relationships between countries or medical fields.

And amidst this pandemic caused due to COVID 19 the medical facilities, the medical and paramedical staff have been playing a very imperative role in every human being's life.

Now you may be wondering, I began with the 21st century and suddenly I'm leaping to COVID 19 and medical teams, but my dear friends I'm trying to make you people connect the dots.

Since we live in this century it becomes our vital responsibility that each one of us contribute to the well-being of mankind.

Every one of us is running behind the statistical facts, the number of deaths caused worldwide, the reason behind the spread of this pandemic, cure for the disease, so on and so forth and why not also – after all this has been wiping out lives of so many people out there.

But has anyone given a thought about the mental disturbances it would have given to some exceptional people???

I don't mean All but still I mentioned SOME and those can vary from hundreds to millions as well which isn't something worth appreciation for a healthy society.

They may be victims of Depression, Anxiety, OCD (obsessive compulsive disorder) or any other mental issues which might not concern other people but can be a major point of concern for these people.

And these are also some aspects to which a glance of attention should be given too, because they also contribute to the sustenance of mankind.

Now the point is How to overcome these issues and how to aware people about this?!

I personally and strongly believe that the best way to overcome this is to Firstly, remain POSITIVE cause positivity not only transmits the positive vibes around you making the surrounding amicable, hearty and lively but also sends a magnetic power to the universe which in return multifolds and come back.

Secondly, I feel that we should try to clear all the misconceptions the majority of people have regarding such mental issues. They should understand that they are no different from them and that these are those things that can happen to anyone in the world and can come to your life as an Uninvited guest, thereby it becomes our basic priority to give them the space they deserve rather than humiliating them or making them feel uncomfortable!

At the end, I would just conclude by saying that World is a really marvellous place to reside in and it becomes even more charming and magnificent when the inhabitants living here live with more harmony and affection and not by developing a feeling of superiority or inferiority complex against each other.

As someone has very wisely said:

"Through our eyes the universe is perceiving itself, through our ears the universe is listening to its harmonies.

We are the witnesses through which the universe becomes conscious of its glory or its magnificence".

Gunjan Pandey

SHE GOT HER THRONE

She still somewhere regrets,

Because she loved you,

She faced so many difficulties alone,

She alone still sweats,

She was ignored, she was rejected,

She was disrespected and misdirected,

She faced everything alone,

Not a single person came,

When she was in difficulty,

That made her stronger,

That made her realize, that her soul is unbroken, she now carries her heart with a smile, she went alone miles,

She did hard work, made her parent's proud, by sacrificing her sleep, her so called friends, whom she once believed, And

Now, she finally got her deserved throne!

Harsha Gehlani

प्यार

फिल्मों में भी चलता हैं और हक़ीक़त में भी

सब लोग इसे कहते हैं प्यार,

कोई तो करता हैं एक दफ़ा

तो कोई करता हैं बार-बार।

कोई इकरार को मानता हैं प्यार

तो कोई इनकार को मानता हैं प्यार,

कोई इंसान से करता हैं प्यार

तो कोई भगवान से करता हैं प्यार।

कोई मतलब जानकर करता है प्यार

तो कोई बिना मतलब जाने करता हैं प्यार,

कोई अपनों से करता हैं प्यार

तो कोई परायों से करता हैं प्यार।

कोई दोस्त से करता हैं प्यार

तो कोई दुश्मन से करता हैं प्यार,

कोई पैसे से करता हैं प्यार

तो कोई प्यार से करता हैं प्यार।

किसी को हैं सुख से प्यार

तो किसी को हैं दुःख से प्यार।

Himanshu Rawat

CHANGE

Change, not for them,

But for yourself.

Change, only if you feel

it's making you

Exemplary.

Change, not when you can

but when you must.

Change, only when your

Body desires.

Change, only when you're

Ready to change.

Change, only if it doesn't

Change YOU.

the idea of YOU shall remain.

Change, because it's

More than just a part of life.

Change can give you

A more lovable life.

Hoshita Sharma

A POET'S POEM

I travel around

throughout the world.

Through the land of mist,

To sea of words.

I can see

through the darkness.

I can hear

a broken soul's cry.

I can feel the beauty of pain

I incarcerate many

emotions within myself,

Waiting for opportunities to be written.

Wandering here and there

I take inspirations,

From blooming buds

to setting sun.

I endeavour to put life in my lines

that reaches readers

heart inside out.

I see the world

With a different perspective

My imagination

Is what keeps me 'round.

My pen bleeds words

Woven into sentences

A basket of emotional

Instances.

You see sunsets

I see all those broken

Heart that cried on its onset

You see rain

I hear the voices behind

It's pain.

Many times, people misinterpret me.

Thinking I'm a loner,

I'm not a loner,

I like to be alone.

Reading and

rereading my thoughts.

People search in dictionary

finding meanings to my words

Huh!

But who 'll tell 'em?

a poet's words cannot

be found in a dictionary.

Look at the irony here.

Dictionaries are meant to find words.

But it cannot find mine.

It's just my beginning,

with never ending end.

I'm a poet,

and it's my trend.

Isha Sharma

I'm a poet,

and it's my trend.

THE UNBROKEN

There is a brokenness;

Out of which comes the unbroken,

A shatteredness;

Out of which blossoms the unshatterable.

There is a misery;

Beyond all the grief which leads to joy,

And a delicacy;

Out of whose depth emerges the strength.

There is vast connotation;

Out of which the words yield me to the hollow
space,

That one spark makes me pass with each loss;

Out of that darkness.

There is a deep cry;

Beyond which comes the small drops of tears,

And an echo;

Out of whose forgettable and ignorable lines.

Inner in my heart;

There is a book full of memories of you,

Which I often open;

To check a part of you missing in my life,

I'm ready to say those lovely words;

Whenever you come to me and only me.

Ishita Chatterjee

RAIN OF LOVE

With it brings thousands of memories,

Reminiscence of you and me becoming us.

Each drop carries love,

Strong enough to touch the ground of
misunderstanding,

Only for it to shout louder.

Symbolizing love is greater.

The dark clouds depict all those fights we've had.

The showers are our tears,

Of the times when we cried so hard to meet each
other.

The essence of sand reminds me of your lavender
perfume,

The dew drops floating on leaves,

Flashed back to the time of our first date,

How my heart skipped a beat,

Every time you held my waist!

My heart floated when our lips were about to melt
with each other.

While our spirits relaxed, the pace of showers
increased every single time,

Catching my breath.

My soul turned green, When the flower of love
touched the surface of cervix.

Roaring thunder conveys the pleasurable pain,

Which every single flowing drop gave us.

And when the crystal-clear droplet freed from the
cascade,

Nature had come to a halt.

Those dark clouds smiled into blue sky.

Once again, rain of love reminded me every
osculate of ours.

Jahnavi Morge

RELATIONSHIP

The word formed of twelve letters,

Doesn't simply mean a bond,

Rather it's a bag full of emotions,

A rapport between two people.

Where one has to respect the other,

Where only love cannot keep it alive

But trust, freedom and compromises,

Are evenly to be shared.

Where time plays a crucial role,

If allotted duly,

Makes it stronger or else gets smashed.

Jharnashree Deka

पहला प्यार

जब मिलती हैं निगाहे उससे तो सब कुछ धुंधला लगता हैं

आती नहीं नींद और ख्यालों उसके फिर वो जगता है

जैसे लगता हैं सब कुछ सुहाना हैं,

उसके सिवा नहीं किसी का दिल मे आना हैं

दिखने के लिए उसको किसी बहाने से उसके घर जाना हैं

और हो जाता उसका वो दीवाना हैं।

फ़िर बात करने के लिए किसी बहाने से हिम्मत जुटाना,

फ़िर हिम्मत करके उससे बात करना, बात करके अपने इश्क़ का
इज़हार करना

और सातवे आसमान मे ख़ुद को पाना।

जब अपने दिल - ओ-अज़ीज़ को पा लेना

उससे सारी बाते करना, उसकी फ़िक्र जाताना ,

उसको प्यार भरे नामों से पुकारना

अपनी हमेशा पलकों पे बिठाना |

अगर कुछ दफ़े के लिए बात ना करें तो नाराज़गी जाताना

उसकी मासूमियत पे सब कुछ हार जाना

नाराज़गी भुलाकर उसको सीने से लगाना,

उसकी पसंद की सारी चीज़े करना

उसको खोने से डरना,

होता हैं कुछ अलग ही भूत सवार

ऐसा होता हैं पहला प्यारा

Kalamkaar

TRUE LOVE

There were a boy and a girl who love each other too much but they hadn't told anyone. They promised each other that they won't leave and hurt each other in any situation. They help each other in every difficulty and enjoyed happy times together and they also promised that they will live together and also die together.

Once they went to the highway for a long drive. They enjoyed there a lot. There was a bridge, waterfall and Mountains.

They went to the bridge; they both were talking with each other. Suddenly bridge got damaged and both fell in the water. Their family searched them a lot but they didn't find them.

And that's known as TRUE LOVE.

They promised each other and also completed that.

Krishna Motwani

LOVE: A RARELY APPREHENDED_EMOTION

"Love all, trust a few and do wrong to none"- As
William Shakespeare said,

Affection, compassion and good will integrated to
one,

Is of what love is made.

Care taken and Sacrifices done out of love shouldn't
be mingled with responsibility,

It's the strength of affection that shows our ability

To decode one's mind's needs,

Just without any words by them spoken

One gets the zeal to repair the loved ones' heart
broken

Through healing words and helpful deeds.

This material world is foolish to tie,

With the sacred emotion of "love",

Their expectations high.

Love should not be attached to a purpose or a cause,

When purpose is over, flow of the so-called love
will pause.

Pure love is as selfless as love of God

For us which has no measuring rod.

His kindness for a murderer and Saint is same,

For atheist behaviour He never blames.

He does for everyone what is right

He punishes the sinner for his reconciliation and for justice guides the righteous to fight.

Divine love carries only positive energy,

He makes punishment and forgiveness work in synergy.

Sometimes His tests are too harsh and cruel

All He wants us to turn into a unique jewel.

It's impossible for worldly human to love all living beings in such a way,

Our materialistic desires, misunderstandings and shallowness keeps us away

From realising the genuineness of love,

It's Serenity, optimism, auspiciousness and

Soothing nature as peaceful and White as a Dove.

Don't lose hope if none loves you in this world

Even the biggest sinner who repents and corrects himself is embraced by Angels in heaven by singing the Holy Heralds.

Kritee Adhikary

SCARED

I am scared to love again,

Maybe scared to be loved this time.

You have my love,

Are you sure moving on isn't a crime?

My heart is becoming more like you,

It has lost beats of mine.

But my pieces are scattered

Can you give me time?

Will, you wait,

Or you'll leave like him.

Should I trust you,

Or I'll lose you in a blink.

Will, you hold my hand,

Whenever I will fall.

Or you'll treat me like trash,

And let my heart crash over a stall.

See I am scared to love,

Will, you adore my flaws,

Or I am just a bait

To satisfy your claws?

I am scared to be loved,

Will you love me for who I am,

Or I have to change?

I don't if all of this sounds strange,

I know I am scared

But if you'll be honest.

I can give my heart a try.

I can love again

if you want to be there for the rest of my life.

Laya

BROKEN YET BEAUTIFUL SOUL

I trusted you but you broke my trust.

I Prayed for your happiness, but you prayed for my tears.

I wrote love letters for you, but you whirled it to breakup letters.

I gave you gifts as a memory (symbol of love too) but you just treated them as Only gifts.

I loved you with my heart, but you pretended as if you love me.

I loaded your eyes with love, but you loaded my eyes with tears.

I swivelled your stone heart into alive with my love, care but you twirled my heart into a broken heart.

I filled your heart with my love, but you filled my heart with broken emotions.

I fought with the entire world to be with you, but you fought with me for every silly reason.

I blame everyone to make you right, but you blamed me to prove that everyone is right, and I am wrong.

I thought to die for you, but you killed me with your words, behaviour.

I craved only for being with you, but you left me to be with others.

You promised me that you will never hurt and doubt me but you always end-up in hurting and doubting me.

I said every truth to you, but you lied everything.

I shared everything with you, but you hid everything from me and shared with someone...!!

My heart turned to a broken heart and stone heart.

My smile turned into tears etc,

I thought all these make me hate you but instead of hating you it started for praying your happiness

Then I realised my love is "TRUE LOVE" and it never ends as you became my soul and world.

Mallela Ravikumar Jayasudha

SOLITAIRE

A small lass

She was never asked

toys chosen or

Benedict picked

Her youth

Hidden in veils

She longed for freedom of the winds.

Silently she sat in a corner

Her fears all encompassed within.

Her eyes filled with tears

As the fire seething

On charcoal.

The winds of change she allowed to envelope her

Flying embers in her heart

She arose

from the blackened hearth, the smouldering fires of
pain and expectations broken

But a glittering solitaire.

Meera Bhansali

तू ना हो तो

कि तू ना हो तो क्या जीना है मेरी ज़िन्दगी का

तू लफ्ज़ है ठहरा हुआ बस मेरी बातों का

तू ही तो बस किस्सा है मेरी जज्बातों का।

तू ही तो मुकहृमा है मेरी हर कोर्ट- कचहरी का

कि तू ना हो तो क्या जीना है मेरी ज़िन्दगी का।

तू ही तो मंज़िल है मेरी राहों कि

तू ही तो कहानी है मेरी रातों की

तू ही कमजोरी है मेरे जिस्म कि

तू ही तो आवाज़ है मेरी बातों की।

तू समा गया है मुझ में इस कदर कि तू ना हो तो अब क्या जीना है
मेरी ज़िन्दगी का।

Megha Mehra

NOSTALGIA OF SCHOOL
(Heart Touching)

Kabhi pehli baar school jaane mein darr lagta tha,

Aaj har rasta khud hi chunte hai..

Kabhi mummy-papa ki har baat sacchi lagti thi,

Aaj unhi se jhooth bolte hai..

Kabhi chhoti si chot kitna rulati thi,

Aaj dil toot jata hai phr bi sambhal jaate hai..

Pehle dost bas saath khelne tak yaad rehte the,

Aaj kuch dost jaan se zyada pyare lagte hai..

Ek din tension ka meaning maa se puchna padta tha,

Or aaj tension soulmate lagta hai..

Ek din tha jab pal mein ladna, pal mein manana to
roz ka kam tha,

Aaj ek baar jo juda hue toh rishte tak kho jate hai..

Sachi, zindagi ne bahut kuch sikha diya tha.

Na jaane rabb ne humko itna jaldi bada kyun bana
Diya.

Nainik Mehta

BYGONE LOVE

In the smoke fall,

Before the nightfall,

With farewell of the sun,

And welcoming of the moon,

A new- love saga burned

Beneath the skin of tree's heart,

And warbling of flock in mist,

Touchwood of pristine souls,

To feel the jovial love,

Melted with warm hands.

Oh! Reviving my bygone days,

Reinvigorated with untold memories.

Weather was mild, day was romantic,

Leaned out of the window,

Waited just to have a look,

Stunned me from the backwards,

A gleeful moment by ripping out,

Beyond any worrisome,

Extravagantly kissed like a lost soul,

Sprouted a new-born fascination,

Hugged as the therapy of smile.

Being in togetherness was sheen,

But some love stories are never meant to be
together.

Slumber nights with dreamy cosmos house,

Surmounting from fragment love gift,

Soft music sucking pain through rustling leaves,

Staying above the sky to see his smile.

Still waits in the veranda,

To listen his vehicle's sound,

Staring intently to the burning path,

Just to have an apparent for sore eyes.

Separation in togetherness,

Aberration in togetherness,

Just expressing joyous love,

Without telling each other,

Without meeting each other.

Nikita Dutta

BROKEN HEARTS

They loved. Society sucked. They loved hard. Society fucked. No one going to love their life. But love carries dreams and memories which have to be done in front of this world. Thus, they sacrificed a lot. But they were imposing to give off. They weren't broken. They just let each other go. It's all about broken hearts and their unbroken soul.

Padmapriya. S

LITTLE GREY BUBBLES

Once upon a summer, I met my rain shower.

Came with a growling thunder, who left me to
wonder.

Mended his lightning bolts, made it his shining
armour.

Kept him warm and taint, away from the rumour.

'Storms aren't loved, they are just vowed,

To drain out your love.'

While I calmed his storm, he blew me a grey
bubble.

Through my fingertips, and into my skin's rubble.

Little grey bubbles, inside my heart.

I went back to the tomb, to bring him back home.

To save him the doubles of his parents' scorn.

Little grey bubbles calmed down the troubles.

Stayed up late and watched him grow.

An old tad lad, perfect and flawed.

Yet he shouts, over my scars.

'Please grow up, you're just blind storm!'

Little grey bubbles, inside my heart.

Lost in its way, to save the later spark.

Pavana Praveen

CHOCOLATE BOY

Hey Niku, the chocolate boy.

Infinite memories with you man.

As I was your favourite toy:

The sister of your clan.

Silly of me considering rain,

As signalling by nature

Meeting my killer of pain,

The ultimate lecture.

Foolish were my eyes,

And so was my skin,

That could not notice your lies,

When my hand was pierced by your pin.

Does love always means my sacrifice?

Will you ever notice.

Or at least realise.

That you killed my compromise.

Pragyan Panda

ROSES OF LOVE

Oh! Those roses of love,

Those roses still bleed

With a hope to get cured

Like the tears of my eyes,

And my heart still bears the pain,

With a hope, that you'll return.

Those stale red-magenta roses

Lost its fragrance in your absence.

There is no more sweetness,

In the honeyed petals of those roses.

It's no more blooming my soul,

But still charm my heart with joy.

Each mushy petal once narrated our love,

Has now became a castle of grief.

And it engulfs my beats into the tunnel of sorrow.

Those roses are now just a bouquet of hope

To console this despair soul that one day,

The essence of smile will glitter your descending
life.

Ritu Jha

SELF LOVE

Accepting myself as the most beautiful being.

Accepting my flaws as they are a beautiful part of
me.

Hold myself to higher standards of being a better
person.

Never change myself for someone unless that
someone is me.

Making me my first priority.

Loving the real me.

Rituparna Sarangi

HAPPY BROKEN SOUL

You once told me to change myself for you,

Yes, I have finally changed for you.

I am finally a changed person,

Not the old one but a new broken soul.

I have stopped complaining and started adjusting.

Adjusting for things which was never worthy to me.

I have stopped thinking and expecting things which
were never mine,

It's better to forget and accept the reality.

Now, I have stopped being happy and started being
sad for small reasons.

Can you see how much you changed me?

I am now a happy me with a broken soul.

Rohit Barman

LOVE THAT IS COMPLETE

They have not met yet, despite being a part of each
other, without knowing.

He was not able to meet her so he sent a letter
scared it will reach to her or not.

When she read the letter, she was elated while
reading the letter.

She met him in the dress he described, he was
searching her and finally they found each other as if
the time stopped.

She went to him and asked for the other half of the
letter, he proposed her in his first part and wrote her
answer as yes but cut it again, he was embarrassed
and looking down.

She kissed him on his cheeks and spoke " you are
lucky, I wanted it or you would be dead by now "

He kissed her back and said " that's how you kiss"

Roopali Purohit

ANKAHE ALFAAZ

Uska kehna bhi sahi

Par mea sunne walo mea kaha

Uska bartav bhi sahi

Par mea sehne walo mea kaha

Apni hi dhun mea yun behta hi gaya

Aur usko apne ye alfaz suna hi naa saka

Aur main karta bhi kya

Kuch akal se kacha bhi toh tha

Par uske jane ke baad thehra bhi toh raha

Ki ek din wo wapas aayegi

Aur uske sath behne ka dhang bhi batlayegi

Lekin uss Raah par uska deedar mumkin nahi

Kyuki main hamesha tha galat aur uska kehna sahi

Bas iss umeed mea aaj bhi jee raha hu

Ki ek baar toh ye alfaaz wo kisi naa kisi se sun payegi.

Rupal Kehmani

A SHORT LOVE STORY

Isn't it too soon for this feeling,

As I dreamed about kissing your palm hand.

Isn't it too soon for this feeling,

As I listened to your favourite band.

Isn't it too strange for a love,

As I let out the me who's been hiding in the ashes.

Isn't it too strange for a love,

As I ignored time but yet the truth smashes.

Isn't it too soon for this pain,

As I cried out a hundred years in a day.

Isn't it too soon for this pain,

As I draw a road and lost the way.

Isn't it too soon to let go,

As I walked through you and did not hug your eyes.

Isn't it too soon to let go,

As I smile in front of the mirror seeing that part of
you in me dies.

Safa Auoissi

PHILOSOPHY OF LOVE

Love is just a four-letter word,

Until someone comes into your life, to give it a
meaning.

Someone who makes you feel like a happy bird,

And gives rise to a new beginning.

Love is so pure, so simple,

But people make it complicated.

Some fall for a smile, some fall for a dimple,

Love for the looks is so overrated.

Love is not just a thing,

That exists between people in a relationship.

It also defines the invisible string,

That exists in the bond of friendship.

For some, Love is a feeling,

For others, it's just a game.

Sometimes, it helps in healing,

Other times, you are put to shame.

Don't be afraid to love people,

In the fear of not being loved back.

Don't let the hurt make you feeble,

And don't let your red heart turn into black.

Love a little more, lie a little less,

Keep it passionate and pure,

Don't make it a mess,

Or don't make someone endure.

Love does not always mean staying together,

You need to sacrifice sometime,

It's all about the care and respect for each other,

Even if it hurts, do not name it as a crime.

People always crave for true love,

And strive hard to find a perfect mate.

Falling for the imperfections is real love,

I hope everyone realizes this, before it's too late.

Sakshi Patankar

MY LOVE

In the rain when there is passion

In the rain when there is passion

In the longing when things to see

There is something magical about you

When you are with me

Your love will remain with me

Your love will remain in prime to see

It won't change at all I don't have things in mind

I know that I am in love with you

Love being so prime

Baby your love defines me in life

Without you I won't survive

Baby I am so in love with you

Love that is my destiny

I love you so much pretty.

Sana Tambe

PLANE

Those mistakes of mine,

never let me sit quite for some time,

I wonder , where was I lost?

When that moment just went endorsed.

I feel it was nothing more than a nightmare,

But still, it affects straight to my share,

I sit quite for long wondering the cause,

Perhaps end up by blaming me off course.

She held me for long,

Maybe just to make me strong,

One day I could bear the pain,

Letting her go into vain.

I know things went wrong,

It could be corrected along,

But neither I step-up nor you,

And that's where happiness left our home.

I wish in some story we will be again together,

Holding each other until September,

Forgetting all the grudges and pain,

Our love will again find a plane.

Shantanu Srivastava

AN ELEGY

My heart is now a barren field

Where no flowers grow anymore

It screams out in despair

But reaches to no one's ear.

My soul is now a lost vendor

Exhausted and needs to be healed

Wandering from one way to the other

Searching back its way to home.

My soul is now tired and broken

Losing all its musings and strains

I looked through the window for one last time

On finding no hope, no light, I chose my end bed of
dead flowers.

Sharmistha Kar

TIME-LESS LOVE

She was not at all pretty, but her eyes seem
modest...

he had love her for her simplicity

he had love her for her peaceful mind

he had loved her because of her simple and caring
nature

he never judged because of her dark colour or of her
specs

in his eyes she was beautiful by her heart

he was always with her even after her parents left
her

he loved her innocence, her soul

in his eyes she was the unique one

he loved her for helpful nature

he loved her for her naughty words

he loved her of being her,

coz, she was different from all

I can see his love, a time - less love

Sheetal Patel

HER REFLECTION

In the mirror,

She saw a reflection,

That shows her herself,

That reflection said to her,

To be stronger for once more.

To look at these scars,

The marks of burning,

Remembering the moment again,

That bottle of acid,

When he threw it at her.

Presently, these scars are crying loud,

Asking her if she still have the ability,

To love herself as earlier,

Also asked if she can stand by her own,

To fight back to those attackers,

And the one who said he loved her.

To take a stand for all those victims,

She heard all those phrases,

Her broken soul whispered,

obviously, she heard.

Shikha Malik

LOVE FROM MOON AND BACK

There's nothing I could ever say & nothing I could
do,

To let you know just how much love is in my heart
for you!

The angels sing when you are near.

Within your arms I have nothing to fear.

You always know just what to say.

Just talking to you makes my day.

When I say I love you, please believe it's true.

When I say goodbye, promise me you won't cry.

You are the sun that shines brightly throughout my
day.

You are the moon that shimmers throughout my
night.

But now I am broken from inside

My love for you was so precious, a love which was
true.

A love that comes from me just to you.

But you never trusted me & broke me from every
bit of my heart.

I ended it and don't know how to clear it at all.

We planned our future as if we have a clue.

I never wanted to lose you.

I wanted you to be my hubby & I wanted to be your
wife.

I wanted to be with you for the rest of my life.

For you the love which I stopped to show,

Actually, abandoned me to live like a happy soul.

Shreya Gupta

PYAR TO PYAR HAI

Pyar to pyar hai,,

Fir vo pita ke sang ho ya maa ke sang,,

Maa ka pehli bar dekhke yu khushi ke aansu sang
Hume dekhna Aur kai br Hume yu daat dena,,

Pyar hi to hai,,

Class me top karne ki khushi se pita ka Sina chauda
hojana orr fail hone pe samjhana sab pyar hi to hai,,

Pyar pyar hai,,

Ruthna bhi Usike sang orr thodi hi der me usse
dherrr saari baate Krna sb pyr hi to hai,,

Uske Cchod jaane pe bhi usse beintehaa Mohabbat
krna,,

Pyar hi to hai,,

Pyar pyar to pyar hai.

Shreya Sirsam

ETERNAL LOVE

Tenderness in my heart,

You are an important part,

The one I adore the most,

And who is close to the innermost.

My love for you grew,

Through and through,

Neither ending nor less,

For this I'm always blessed.

You are my sunshine,

Whose rays are only mine,

Without you my life is dark,

Feels like days are falling apart.

You are the one who makes me complete,

With you my life is bittersweet,

For all the good times I have now,

I would try to cherish them anyhow.

I love you to the end of my life,

Hoping to be together with you afterlife,

You are always in my prayers,

Wishing to spend my life with you with much love
and care.

Simi Chutia

FEELS OF LOVE

Love, the most beautiful of all topics,

the question with most struggled answers.

Love is like a fascinating and alluring tale that is
bound by no endings and no beginnings.

Love- can never be explained, neither in the shortest
way possible nor in all the books of the world in the
longest way possible.

People say that you must trust, be loyal and support
your love but that is wrong.

"Love" itself is the one word for: -

Loyalty

Commitment

Trust

Faith

Support

Care

Passion

Intimacy

Equanimity

Compassion, among other things that all come from within, you don't "have to" but you like to do all that for love.

There's an intoxicating feeling you have about

anyone irrespective of where they come from.

Love is the purest form of care and respect

which are nowhere near infatuation and lust.

There's no answer to "why you love that person",

you just do, and your soul knows it from the moment you see them.

Love is free from greed and injustice.

There's no thinking process, you just have

your beloved in your mind all the time.

The invaluable instincts of time, truth,

trust, peace, and confinement are the

undisputed guards of the palace of love.

Love is a two-way thing; you give, and you take but there are no bigger expectations. You don't think in love, you just bring out what your heart suggests. Yes, you're possessive and insecurities arise because you know that the world around isn't kind enough. Here's when the trust and loyalty come into play.

Yes, there are tons of unexpected and unwanted situations that tend to or force you to stay away from the one you love but that's not justice. First of all, if it's meant to be, then it'll happen anyway, no matter how many people or situations interfere, but whenever needed, you should take stand of each-other.

Don't make promises that you can't keep because everyone knows what they can or can't do, so it's better to stay away than destroying an otherwise happy person if you really are in love and don't want anything that hurts. If you're with someone then please have the guts to accept that fact in front of other people, i.e., know to make others know that you're taken. If someone else tends to come close to you and if you let them be, then my friend you're damned and so are those people around you. If you start liking some other person then do tell. Secrets and lies do no better.

Don't let the fights stay unheard or unsolved.

Remember that why you are with that person in the first place.

Should I hold you with bare hands,

or tie you with silk threads to me?

Should I say those I love yous,

or make you look into the eyes of me?

Should I listen to you undeniably?

or make you hear words from lips of me?

Should I keep asking how much you care,

or feel it against the heart of thee?

Should I get drowned into your kisses,

or forget all in those warm hugs of thee?

Should I compare my hands with yours,

or just let you take me into the arms of thee?

Should I live out all my present for you,

or plan that whole future with you of me?

You're surrounded by these thoughts sometimes,
then it's necessary for you to take a deep breath and
try to understand.

Keep it simple and your life will be beautiful
forever.

Love with all your heart and soul.

Simran Dhingra

एक शाम तुम फिर आना

एक शाम तुम फिर आना, हर लम्हा हम जी जाएंगे

बीतता वक्त,भले चलती घड़ी

हाथों में हाथ थामे हम ठहर जाएंगे,

आज की तेज़ मचलती लहरों में,

हम कल की कश्ती चलाएंगे।

साथ बैठकर एक दूजेके

हम वह पल फ़िर से दोहराएंगे,

एक शाम तुम फिर आना, हम वो सारे वादे निभाएंगे।

शोर भरे इस शहर में हम

खामोशी से तुम्हे पाएंगे,

जीया है जिसे ख्यालो में बार-बार,

वह पुरानी सफर पर जाएंगे।

प्यार हुआ था जिस पल हमें,

वह लम्हा महसूस कराएंगे।

एक शाम तुम फिर आना,हम नए डोर से बंध जाएंगे।

बात अधूरी ना रहे, हर पल को वक्त से चुराएंगे ।

अल्फाजो से बयां करके नहीं,

हम आंखों से लब्ज सुनाएंगे।

छुटी थी कहानी जहा से अपनी,

फिर वहीं से आगे बढ़ाएंगे। एक शाम

Srujan Hiral Gaurang

I MISS YOU, MY LOVE

I miss those endless talks,

talks depleted with the love and ecstasy, the way

you made me pour out of my heartaches.

I miss those minutes of passion,

your eyes were fixed upon mine

and where I breathed the scents of our intermingled

souls.

I miss those endless chats, vibrating phone and the

overwhelming happiness we shared being distanced.

I miss those cloudy days, when the rain drenched

you all over,

watching you in the wet shirt, and the way my lips

stood motionless to kiss you over and over.

I miss those small evening meets, when you return

to me after long yet your presence would heal all

my unwanted pain in split seconds.

I miss those hands which trembled touching me smoothly and the depth of your love seems never ending.

I miss those times when you smiled at me, your smile swearing me of the love you depict for me forever.

I am missing every moment of our lives together, missing your presence which makes me bloom, missing not only our far-gone memories but also the person whom I love the most.

Subhrajyoti Nanda

HOPE: A FAITHFUL WISH

Hope from the universe's anticipation of good,

wished everything will be okay but sometimes it's okay not to be okay.

Nothing is coincidence because destiny knows its undeviating road that we find confiscated.

The universe had bonded us together because we comprised of the identical stardust.

"I had died every day waiting for you", these lines remind me of your unexplainable essence.

Even though we are far away but I can feel the soulful essence of your vibes.

When I think of you, it left me stagnant but you will always remember my essence with those pleasant vibes of winds.

'GOODBYE ' might be the end of something beautiful but that 'FOREVER ' sows the seed of something even more attractive.

The seeds are in the dormant stage and that creates negative vibes until when only the universe knows.

You had met me via your destiny, but I had met you because of my fate.

It felt like we are the parallel lines of universe who can walk together forever but can't meet.

Your memories leave me emotionless and overemotional at the same time.

The affection of your words will remain forever in all four chambers of my heart.

Your essence will flow in my veins even after my 'goodbye'!

Suhani Singh

BROKEN HEART MAY BE BEAUTIFUL

Pleasure of love lasts but a moment. Pain of love lasts a lifetime. The heart will break but broken live on. It is strange how often a heart must be broken before the years can make it wise. Perhaps someday I'll crawl back home, beaten, defeated. But not if I can make stories out of my heartbreak, beauty out of sorrow. The saddest thing about love is that not only that it cannot last forever, but that heartbreak is soon forgotten. Relive-Remember-Re-found these are found to be hell without you, but you don't understand or can't want to understand. A broken heart is just the growing pains necessary so that you can love more completely when the real thing comes along. The best and most beautiful things in the world cannot be seen or even touched - they must be felt with the heart, but it's broken and now it's time to rebuild it to beautiful.

Go on a wrong path in a right way...

And some to…

Go on a right path in a wrong way...

Path... Are far

Way... Are far

Miles to go... Without you.

Miles to Walk away... Without you. Darkness is the best way to keep myself their... for a while. After that a light will come as a sparkle star to rebuild my broken heart.

Swapna S. Tripathy

RAISED WITH RESILIENCE

While this world,

and its crooked crannies -

ceaselessly endeavoured -

to slay me apart and whole,

it was only that core -

of my being,

the very one that had been -

raised with resilience to resist -

every worldly woe,

that pulled me together -

to pave an upstanding path,

as the only way to get out -

alive and well.

Tabassum Hasnat

A NIGHT WITH YOU

In the middle of the night,

in the smoke of the ending cigarette,

I'm thinking of you.

Like a wind you slightly touch my soul,

and like a leaf I'm resisting you.

But it is so late until you,

take me to flow with you.

Under the peaceful moonlit sky,

I'm wishing to be one of those stars.

But now I stand with you,

feeling I'm a part of the galaxy in your eyes.

The sky is jealous of your warmth,

as we hold our hands.

The ocean waves throw tiny droplets on us,

making us feel cold,

it feels like the universe has got us together,

as if we are made of the same stardust.

I wish you never leave,

this night feels so dark without you.

But it was time for us to leave,

for me to say to you , "goodbye",

and to this splendid night,

Until we meet again.

Vaishali Bindal

UNIVERSE OF LOVE

Dear love,

Be my sun,

Who will brighten up my dull sparkle.

Be my moon,

Who will guide me through the darkness of life.

Be my shooting star,

Who I wished to come true in this world surrounded
by fake souls

My love,

Join me in my journey to infinity,

Where time is unmeasurable,

Let me hold your hand,

Fly you to the edge of the Earth.

To the borderless universe,

And paint it with the hues of our love.

Vanmitha Anthimoolam

LOVE-THE HEARTBEAT OF HUMANITY

Since time immemorial, its love is inspiring and
uplifting us, while other organisms thrived on
survival instincts, it made us conquer pinnacles of
technology.

The most massive genocides, wars, innovations, and
discoveries all fuelled by love throughout historical
chronology,

Its love which propels us from the darkest abyss and
shines in the most dismal horror like a ray of
sunshine.

Its love which differentiates humans from animals
and provides our miniscule lives a purpose almost
divine,

Often misunderstood for love, is misunderstanding,
infatuation and obsession.

Whereas its love which invigorates us to enjoy
every spectrum of life and get every cell of our
existence beam with ecstasy.

Vishnu Prasad Nair

SHATTERED GLASS

An unimagined dream which left her shattered,

The only thing that mattered,

ended up leaving her scattered.

As the series of questions didn't conclude,

She got numb

To the pain,

To the abuse too.

Restlessness imprisoned her own thoughts as soon
as she invited tranquillity.

No one noticed but,

everything could be felt with her

One stare,

sleepless nightmare,

Unshed tears,

Dried eyes,

Voiceless screams,

Tightened throat,

Shacked soul.

In the end, she became heartless.

She turned unbothered.

Once hurtful,

Converted hurtless.

VOID

आपकी मासूमियत

आपकी मासूमियत का

कोई जवाब नहीं

और इस कदर

आपसे मोहब्बत हुई,

की कोई हिसाब नहीं

और तेरी निगाहों ने

मानो मेरे दिल का

क़त्ल कर दिया,

किसी पे मर के कैसे जीते है

आज तेरी एक

मुसकुराहट ने बता दिया।

की यूँ तो हर पल

जल्दी कटता नहीं

पर जबसे तेरा दिदार हुआ है

मानो मेरे लिए

समय बचता नहीं,

और मेरे हर आने

वाले पल को बस तेरी

ख्वाहिश होती है।

पर जिस पल में भी

तू ना मिली जानेमन

उस पल में दूर दूर तक

खुशियों का भी आगाज़ नही,

और जानेमन आप

पूछती हो कि

हम आपसे मोहब्बत

कितना करते है?

तो यार अब हमें

माफ़ ही करदो

क्यों की हम अपने

मोहबत को बयां कर सके

हमारे पास इतने

भी अलफ़ाज़ नही।

Yasharsh Kiyan

प्यार

अगर मैं कहूँ कि मुझे प्यार है तुमसे

तो तुम मुझे अपना पाओगे क्या?

मेरी सूरत को छोड़

मेरी सीरत से दिल लगा पाओगे क्या?

मेरी मुस्कुराहट के पीछे का दर्द को

मेरे साथ बैठकर बाट पाओगे क्या?

अगर मैं कहूँ कि मुझे प्यार है तुमसे

तो तुम मुझे अपना पाओगे क्या?

मेरी सावली रंगत को छोड

मेरी आँखों में छुपी हुई चमक को पहचान पाओगे क्या?

इस मतलबी दुनिया में

मेरा साथ ना छोड़ने का वादा कर पाओगे क्या?

अगर मैं कहूँ के मुझे प्यार है तुमसे

तो तुम मुझे अपना पाओगे क्या?

मेरे साथ दो पल बैठ

मेरी शायरी में बस पाओगे क्या?

वो खुशनुमा शाम में

बारिशों के बीच ,

मेरे साथ दो घुट चाय की चुस्की लगा पाओगे क्या

अगर मैं कहूँ के मुझे प्यार है तुमसे

तो तुम मुझे अपना पाओगे क्या?

अगर जवाब ना है तो

एक सवाल है मेरा के

मेरे साथ बिताए हुए वो पल

भुला पाओगे क्या?

अगर मैं कहूँ के मुझे प्यार है तुमसे

तो तुम मुझे अपना पाओगे क्या।

Zubia Mariyam

9 789390 724024